Flea and Big Bill

Written by Jill Eggleton
Illustrated by Astrid Matijasevich

Flea saw a hat.
"I will get on this hat,"
said Flea.

Big Bill put on his hat.
He got on the bus.

"I like going on the bus,"
said Flea.

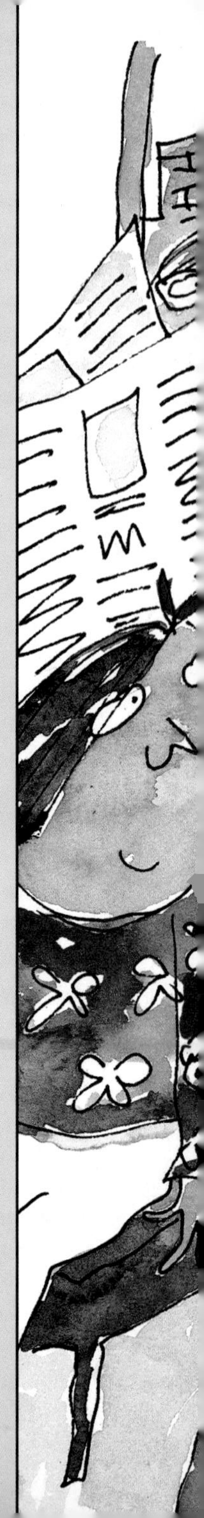

Big Bill went to the mall.

He went to the movies, too.

“I like it on this hat,”
said Flea.

Big Bill went
down the road.

"I will go to sleep,"
said Flea.

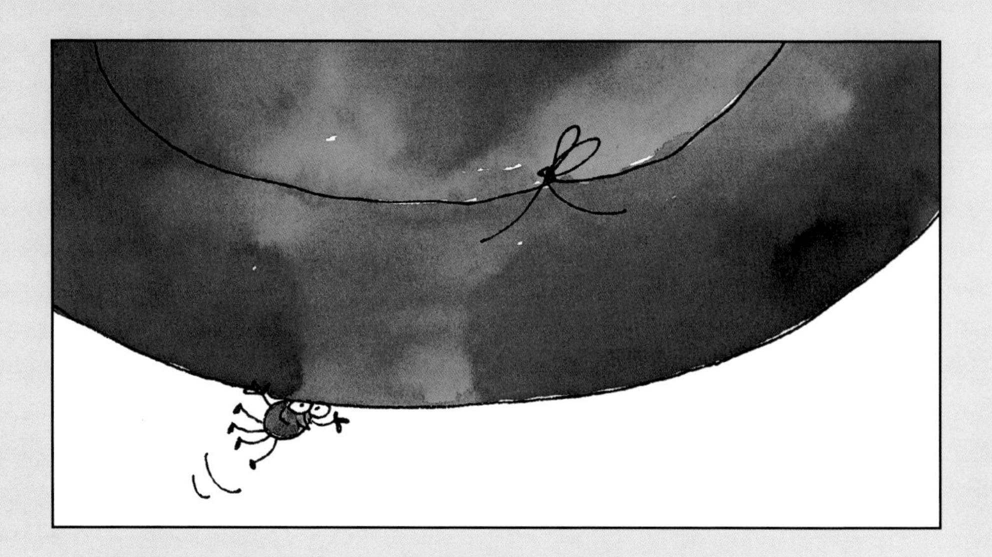

Flea went under the hat.

Big Bill went
scratch, scratch, scratch!

"**Yuck!**" shouted Big Bill.
"A flea is on my head!"

Big Bill went home.
"I will get in the shower,"
he said.

"Oh, no," said Flea.
"I'm going."

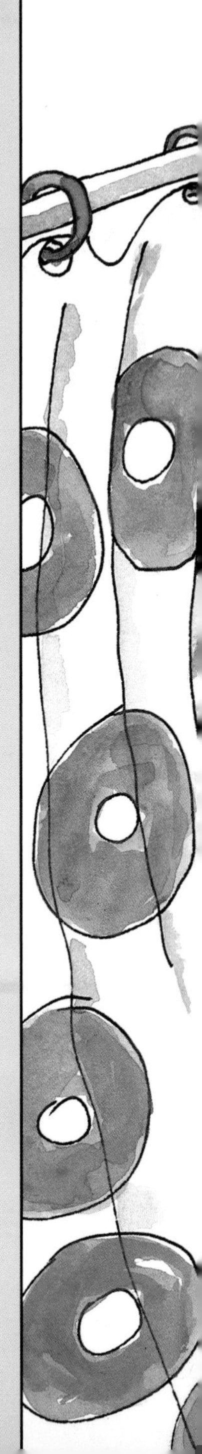

B

Flea went
hop, hop, hop
into Big Bill's bed.
"I will sleep in here,"
said Flea.

A Story Sequence

Guide Notes

Title: Flea and Big Bill
Stage: Early (2) – Yellow

Genre: Fiction
Approach: Guided Reading
Processes: Thinking Critically, Exploring Language, Processing Information
Written and Visual Focus: Story Sequence
Word Count: 119

THINKING CRITICALLY

(sample questions)

- What do you think this story could be about?
- Focus on the title and discuss.
- Why do you think Flea liked going on Big Bill's hat?
- Why do you think Flea went under the hat to go to sleep?
- Why do you think Big Bill went home?
- What do you think might happen when Big Bill gets into bed?

EXPLORING LANGUAGE

Terminology

Title, cover, illustrations, author, illustrator

Vocabulary

Interest words: movies, mall, scratch, shower, home
High-frequency words: saw, his, get, I'm
Positional words: under, on, down, in, into

Print Conventions

Capital letter for sentence beginnings and names (**F**lea, **B**ig **B**ill), periods, commas, quotation marks, exclamation marks